To my brother, Tom Zietlow, a most
excellent uncle to my two daughters
-PZM

For Andrew, always
-AM

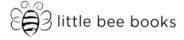 little bee books

An imprint of Bonnier Publishing USA
251 Park Avenue South, New York, NY 10010
Text copyright © 2018 by Pat Zietlow Miller
Illustrations copyright © 2018 by Alea Marley
All rights reserved, including the right of reproduction
in whole or in part in any form. Little Bee Books is a
trademark of Bonnier Publishing USA, and associated colophon
is a trademark of Bonnier Publishing USA.
Manufactured in China   HUH 0518
First Edition
2 4 6 8 10 9 7 5 3 1
ISBN 978-1-4998-0681-6
Library of Congress Cataloging-in-Publication Data
Names: Miller, Pat Zietlow, author. | Marley, Alea, illustrator.
Title: Loretta's gift / by Pat Zietlow Miller; illustrated by Alea Marley.
Description: First edition. | New York: Little Bee Books, 2018. | Summary:
Loretta tries hard to come up with the perfect gift for her beloved baby cousin,
Gabe, but on his first birthday she learns she has already given him something
special. | Identifiers: LCCN 2017048474 | Subjects: | CYAC: Babies—Fiction.
| Gifts—Fiction. | Cousins—Fiction. | Love—Fiction. | Family life—Fiction.
Classification: LCC PZ7.M63224 Lor 2018 | DDC [E]—dc23
LC record available at https://lccn.loc.gov/2017048474
littlebeebooks.com
bonnierpublishingusa.com

Loretta's Gift

Pat Zietlow Miller and Alea Marley

little bee books

Loretta was skipping rope when she heard the news.
Aunt Esme and Uncle Jax were expecting a baby.

There was laughter
and tears
and hugging
and cheers.

"Babies," said Loretta's mother,
"are a celebration."
"Of what?" Loretta wondered.
"Of life. Of love. Of hope,"
said her father.

Loretta looked at Aunt Esme's belly.
Could it hold all that *and a baby?*

Before long, Loretta's world was buzzing with love.
There were, it seemed, lots of ways to celebrate a baby.

Loretta's mother knit fuzzy hats.

Loretta's father bought piles of diapers.

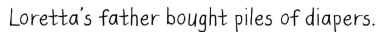

Uncle Jax built a cradle.

And Aunt Esme filled the nursery
with family photos.

There was even a party with presents stacked higher than Loretta's head.

But no gift from Loretta.

"What can I give the baby?"
she asked.

"Nothing, sweetie," said her mother.
"No one expects you to give a gift."
Loretta frowned. That didn't seem right.
She wanted to celebrate too.

So she skipped rope and thought.

She could buy something!
But her penny collection wasn't enough.

She could share something!
But her jump rope wasn't bright and shiny.

She could make something!

But after hours of work, the only thing she'd made was a mess.

Before Loretta knew it, Aunt Esme and
Uncle Jax were home with baby Gabe.
He wore fuzzy hats and soft diapers
and slept in his very own cradle.

There was laughter
and tears
and hugging
and cheers.
Not to mention more gifts.

Loretta stared at Gabe. He had the curliest hair and the tiniest toes. "You are the best baby on the block," she whispered.

"He's the stinkiest, for sure," said Uncle Jax.
"Could you find a diaper?"

Loretta could.

As Gabe grew, Loretta organized his hats,

tickled his toes,

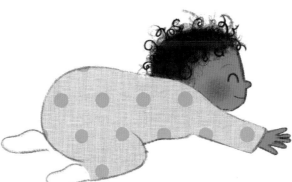

fed him mashed bananas,

and rocked him until he slept.

Soon Gabe smiled whenever he saw Loretta.
Loretta always smiled back and asked,
"Who's the best baby on the block?"

But she never stopped searching for the perfect gift.

Before Loretta knew it,
Gabe's first birthday arrived.

Aunt Esme greeted guests,
Uncle Jax served cake, and
Loretta's parents poured fizzy drinks.
Loretta watched everyone laugh,
hug, and add presents to the pile.

Still, as the pile got taller,
Loretta felt smaller
and smaller
and smaller.

Why couldn't she find a gift for Gabe?

While everyone celebrated, Gabe pulled himself to his feet
and took his first shaky steps. Everyone cheered.

Until Gabe tumbled into
the pile of presents.
He wailed.

Loretta sailed to his side.

She adjusted his hat,
which had slipped over one eye,

rocked him in her arms
until he stopped sobbing,

and tickled his toes until
his sniffles subsided.

Gabe wasn't crying anymore. But he wasn't smiling either.
That didn't seem right.

So Loretta grabbed a bow, stuck it on her head,
and asked, "Who's the best baby on the block?"
Gabe giggled.
And everyone else joined in.

"Well, Loretta," said Aunt Esme, "I think you're the best gift Gabe ever got."

Loretta paused.
Was that true?
She remembered the laughter,
the tears, the hugging, and the cheers.
And all those mashed bananas.

She knew her love was better than anything that came in a box.
And Gabe would never outgrow it — no matter how many birthdays he had.

Then Loretta laughed loudest of all.
Because suddenly, everything was exactly right.
And the best baby on the block thought so too.

31901063628707